Room for a Friend

by Paul Webb
illustrated by John Veeken

⊠Harcourt
SCHOOL PUBLISHERS

Printed in China

ISBN 10: 0-15-350382-3
ISBN 13: 978-0-15-350382-5

Ordering Options
ISBN 10: 0-15-350331-9 (Grade 1 Below-Level Collection)
ISBN 13: 978-0-15-350331-3 (Grade 1 Below-Level Collection)
ISBN 10: 0-15-357405-4 (package of 5)
ISBN 13: 978-0-15-357405-4 (package of 5)

5 6 7 8 9 10   468   15 14 13 12 11 10 09

"Let's play!" said Duck
to her friends.
Her friends ran off
and hid.

Chicken came by
Cow's barn.
"Join me," called Cow.
Chicken did.

Pig came by.
"Please join us," called
Chicken.
Pig did.

Rabbit came by.
"There's always room
for a friend," Pig called.
Rabbit hid.

Duck came by. She saw
Rabbit's back.

Duck looked into the shed.
"It's nice to see you all!"

"Thanks, Rabbit!" called
Duck.
"It's your turn to find us
now!"

Think Critically

1. What did you learn from the story?

2. Which animals were the first and the last to hide?

3. What happened at the end of the story?

4. What made it easy for Duck to find her friends?

5. What game do you enjoy playing with your friends?

 Social Studies

Write Rules Think of a game you play with your friends. Write sentences that tell three rules of the game.

School-Home Connection Tell a family member about the game the animals played. Then play a game with your family.

Word Count: 78

GRADE 1

Lesson 16

WORD COUNT

78

GENRE

Fantasy

LEVEL

See TG or go Online

ISBN-13: 978-0-15-350382-5
ISBN-10: 0-15-350382-3

9 780153 503825

90000

MASTODON
FARM

MIKE KLEINE